Walking Round the Garden

by John Prater

THE BODLEY HEAD
LONDON

Walking roun

he garden,

Like

eddy bear,

One step

wo steps,

Tickle yo

under there.

Walking dow.

he hallway,

Up and u

he stairs,

One step

wo steps,

What

lever bear!

Sitting i

ne bedroom,

What

leepy ted,

All I need i

goodnight kiss

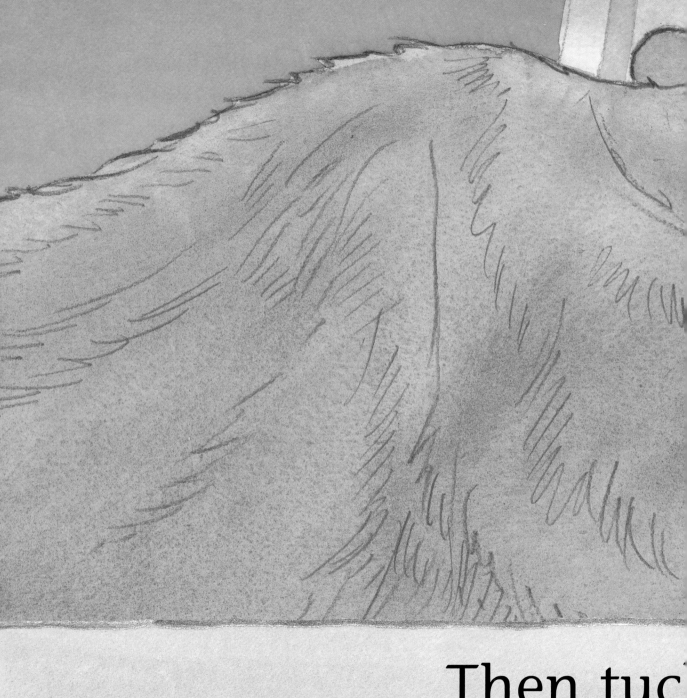

Then tuc